A NOTE TO PARENTS

Congratulations on choosing the best in educational materials for your child. By selecting top-quality McGraw-Hill products, you can be assured that the concepts used in our books will reinforce and enhance the skills that are being taught in classrooms nationwide.

And what better way to get young readers excited than with Mercer Mayer's Little Critter, a character loved by children everywhere? Our First Readers offer simple and engaging stories about Little Critter that children can read on their own. Each level incorporates reading skills, colorful illustrations, and challenging activities.

Level 1 – The stories are simple and use repetitive language. Illustrations are highly supportive.
Level 2 - The stories begin to grow in complexity. Language is still repetitive, but it is mixed with more challenging vocabulary.
Level 3 - The stories are more complex. Sentences are longer and more varied.

To help your child make the most of this book, look at the first few pictures in the story and discuss what is happening. Ask your child to predict where the story is going. Then, once your child has read the story, have him or her review the word list and do the activities. This will reinforce vocabulary words from the story and build reading comprehension.

You are your child's first and most influential teacher. No one knows your child the way you do. Tailor your time together to reinforce a newly acquired skill or to overcome a temporary stumbling block. Praise your child's progress and ideas, take delight in his or her imagination, and most of all, enjoy your time together!

This product has been aligned to state and national organization standards using the Align to Achieve Standards Database. Align to Achieve, Inc., is an independent, not-for-profit organization that facilitates the evaluation and improvement of academic standards and student achievement. To find how this product aligns to your standards, go to www.MHstandards.com.

Mc Graw Hill Children's Publishing

Text Copyright © 2004 McGraw-Hill Children's Publishing.
Art Copyright © 2004 Mercer Mayer.

Send all inquiries to:
McGraw-Hill Children's Publishing
8787 Orion Place
Columbus, OH 43240-4027

Printed in the United States of America.

1-57768-584-9

 A Big Tuna Trading Company, LLC/J. R. Sansevere Book

Library of Congress Cataloging-in-Publication Data is on file with the publisher.

1 2 3 4 5 6 7 8 9 10 PHXBK 08 07 06 05 04 03

The McGraw-Hill Companies

FIRST READERS

Level **3**   Grades **1–2**

CHRISTMAS FOR MISS KITTY

by Mercer Mayer

Mc Graw Hill **Children's Publishing**

Columbus, Ohio

Little Critter's class was having a Christmas party. Everyone was going to get a gift for their teacher, Miss Kitty. *I want to get her the best present ever,* thought Little Critter.

6

Mom took Little Critter shopping in
Critterville. He chose a green scarf. He
used all the money in his piggy bank.
"I hope Miss Kitty likes it," he said.
"Green is her favorite color."

After dinner, Little Critter wanted to wrap Miss Kitty's present.
Just then, he saw Blue tugging at something under the bed. It was the scarf!
"No, Blue!" cried Little Critter.

10

But Blue ran. Little Critter chased Blue.
He grabbed the other end of the scarf.
Blue tugged. Little Critter tugged.
They both tugged until...

…they tore the scarf in half.
"Oh, no! Tomorrow is the Christmas party," said Little Critter. "And my present is ruined."
"Maybe we can fix it," said Mom.

14

Little Critter tried to glue the scarf back together. The glue did not work. So, Little Critter stapled the scarf together instead. Then, Little Sister sprinkled some glitter on it. Blue even tried to help.

"Mom, do you like it?" asked Little Critter.

"I love it," said Mom. "Remember, it's the thought that counts."

But Little Critter was not so sure.

At the party, everyone gave Miss Kitty their presents.

When she opened Little Critter's gift, she smiled. "Thank you, Little Critter. Green is my favorite color," she said.

Little Critter smiled back. "Merry Christmas, Miss Kitty!"

"Merry Christmas, class!" said Miss Kitty.

Word List

Read each word in the lists below. Then, find each word in the story. Now, make up a new sentence using the word. Say your sentence out loud.

Words I Know	Challenge Words
class	favorite
gift	glitter
glue	present
green	ruined
scarf	thought
teacher	wrap

Comprehension Quiz

Answer these questions. Try
not to look back at the story.

Why does Little Critter want to get Miss Kitty
a present?

What color was Miss Kitty's scarf?

How did the scarf get ruined?

How did Little Critter try to fix the scarf?

Who helped Little Critter fix the scarf?

How do we know that Miss Kitty liked the
scarf?

Silent Letters

Sometimes words have letters that are silent. That means that they don't make a sound when the word is spoken. In the word wrap, the letter w is silent.

(w)r a p

Point to the silent letter in each word below.

game

half

climb

write

Action Words

Action words show someone doing something. Point to each action word below.

gift

run

scarf

tug

chase

Word Families

If you change the first letter of each word below, you can make a new word. Say your new words out loud, and then use each one in a sentence.

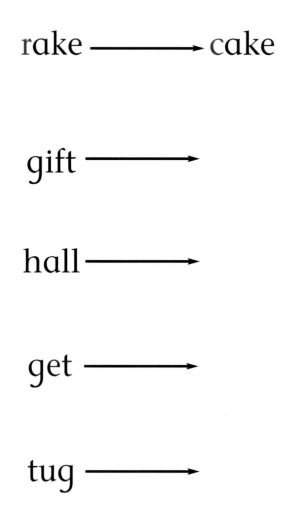

rake ⟶ cake

gift ⟶

hall ⟶

get ⟶

tug ⟶

ABC Order

abcdefghijklmnopqrstuvwxyz

On a separate piece of paper, write each set of words in abc order. Look at the first letter in each word to help you.

green

scarf

bank

- - - - - - - - - - - - -

help

glitter

thought

- - - - - - - - - - -

merry

class

fix

Answer Key

page 19
Comprehension Quiz

1. Little Critter wants to buy Miss Kitty a present for their class Christmas party.
2. Miss Kitty's scarf was green.
3. The scarf got ruined because Blue and Little Critter tore it in half.
4. Little Critter tried to glue and staple the scarf.
5. Mom, Little Sister, and Blue tried to help Little Critter fix the scarf.
6. We know that Miss Kitty liked the scarf because she smiled and said that green was her favorite color.

page 20
Silent Letters

game

half

climb

write

page 21
Action Words

run

chase

tug

page 22
Word Families

Answers may vary. Examples include:

gift   lift, sift

hall   ball, call, fall, mall, tall, wall

get   bet, jet, let, met, net, pet, set, wet

tug   bug, dug, hug, jug, mug, rug

page 23
ABC Order

bank
green
scarf

glitter
help
thought

class
fix
merry

24